Mubu & Mu-Mu

The Little Animal Doctor

Peter Alexander

Order this book online at www.kennebec7.com or www.trafford.com
or email orders@trafford.com

Most Trafford titles are also available at major online book retailers.

Printed in Thailand

ISBN: 978-1-4269-3886-3

Library of Congress Control Number: 2010911119

*Our mission is to efficiently provide the world's finest, most comprehensive book publishing
service, enabling every author to experience success. To find out how to publish your book, your
way, and have it available worldwide, visit us online at www.trafford.com*

Trafford rev. 08/23/2010

 www.trafford.com

North America & international
toll-free: 1 888 232 4444 (USA & Canada)
phone: 250 383 6864 ♦ fax: 812 355 4082

To Lek Chailert and Jodi Thomas
of The Elephant Nature Park,
and to Jokia and Hope,
two elephants who represent
the past and the future

One day when I was six, I was taking care of my baby sister while my mother worked in our vegetable garden.

Suddenly, in the distance, I heard a whistling sound from the forest. It sounded like a noisy laughing thrush, but I knew it was not quite the same as a real laughing thrush bird.

I called back with my own whistle, and then after a few seconds I got a reply. I knew then that it was my grandfather Noom calling me in the language of the laughing thrush.

Suddenly, there he was, coming out of the forest. He had been away for two nights looking for herbs that would help cure the sickness of one of our neighbors. My grandfather knew how to find plants in the forest that could help most of our villagers.

But this time Grandfather Noom brought back something else besides his bag of herbs. In his left arm he carried a small, dark, furry animal.

"What is it? What is it, Grandfather?" I jumped up in excitement and ran to him.

It was a baby gibbon. With such an adorable little face, but frightened and sad!

"What happened to it?" I exclaimed.

Grandfather showed me the tiny animal's hand. There was a bloody hole in the middle of its little palm. "It was stabbed in a trap," he told me.

Grandfather smiled at me with his serious eyes. "Mubu, I believe you can help this baby survive. You are my little animal doctor."

I was so proud to hear him call me an animal doctor, I almost fainted with happiness. Yes! I could do it!

Carefully, he placed the trembling baby in my arms. Those sad, sweet little brown eyes looked into my face. They trusted me. I must not disappoint my grandfather or this fuzzy treasure.

"Before I leave this baby with you, Mubu," he said to me, "there are rules you must obey."

Uh-oh. I looked up at him with my eyes darting. Rules! Ugh.
"What kind of rules, Grandfather?" I asked politely.

He touched a different finger as he announced each rule.

"No name for the gibbon."

"No cuddling the gibbon."

"No gibbon sleeping in your bed."

My face could not hide my disappointment. My grandfather knew how attached I became to my animal friends. I used to cry and fuss whenever he would take the wild animals I helped heal back into the forest.

He knew, too, that the animals usually wanted to stay with me because they had forgotten what their real home was. He always told me that wild animals must return to the forest where Nature intended them to be. "But, Grandfather, they love to be with me."

"This gibbon has a family back in the forest, Mubu," he said.

"Yes, Grandfather," I said, my eyes looking down at the ground, the little gibbon in my arms already holding tighter to my shirt and enjoying the warmth of my body.

While Grandfather Noom began building a wonderful house for the baby, I fed fruit to her. I had watched him gently apply the herbal mixture he had made to help heal the deep wound in the gibbon's hand.

He blew softly on the wound and spoke. "Go away, bad spirit. Go and play in another place. You bring no happiness here."

He built a brilliant crosshatched bamboo home for the baby. It covered two mango trees!

Imagine! The new home completely protected my gibbon, but gave her two trees to swing on with her one good hand and two good feet. Grandfather also built a small door at the bottom so I could come and go when I had to do my doctor's duties.

The baby was very excited to see me each day when I brought food and medicine. She swung down eagerly from her branches to see what I had brought. I fed her fruit and nuts, which she devoured hungrily.

I put medicine on her poor little hand. I blew on her wound the way my grandfather did, and said, "Baby, I love you."

My gibbon then took my hand and copied me. She blew on it and then looked into my eyes. "I love you, too," those eyes seemed to say.

Then, because climbing trees was one of my favorite things, I hopped up on a branch. My baby quickly followed me, her eyes shining as she realized that she had not only a doctor but a playmate, too!

We swung back and forth between the trees, but of course my gibbon was a much faster climber, even with one injured hand.

When everyone was asleep one night, I broke one of Grandfather's rules. I brought my gibbon into my bedroom. The baby was so excited! She began to swing and jump around the room.

"Shhhh!" I told her, putting my finger to my lips.

"Shhhh," the baby mimicked, putting a finger to her lips with a mischievous smile.

I felt like I had a sister my own age to play with and to share my feelings with.

My gibbon would walk around blowing kisses to me. I put my hand over my mouth to keep my giggling quiet. Then she would copy me, covering her mouth and shaking as if she was giggling, too.

I put medicine on her wound and blew on it softly. My gibbon took my hand and licked it tenderly.

I told her, "You must have a name." Uh-oh—another rule. It was too late. That rule flew out the window.

"My name is Mubu," I told my gibbon. "That's because I climb trees like a monkey. So you can become Mu-Mu because you're already a monkey." She made happy noises.

"But don't tell anybody," I warned Mu-Mu. "You're not supposed to have a name." Mu-Mu nodded her head up and down. Then we broke the third rule as we cuddled in my bed.

One morning as I was making my plans for a great adventure, Grandfather Noom came to me and said, "Mubu, do you want to go with me into the forest?"

"Not today, Grandfather, thanks," I told him politely. "I want to play." He understood that six-year-old children love to play, so he waved to me and left for one of his own adventures.

I bent down and entered Mu-Mu's home. She was sitting on a branch studying the palm of her injured hand. It had been getting better and I could tell it was starting to itch. Mu-Mu wasn't sure what to do about an itch.

"Mu-Mu," I told her, "I'll take you for a great adventure if you promise not to make a lot of noise."

Mu-Mu said, "Woo-woo!" excitedly, and jumped down from her branch.

We quietly snuck out of the village and Mu-Mu hesitantly followed me into the forest. She tilted her head back and stared up at the tall trees so much that she fell over backward. Maybe she had forgotten that in the real world there were a lot more trees than the two inside her bamboo home.

We climbed together on that last wonderful day we spent with each other. We chased each other and swung on vines. I felt that she and I were truly soul mates who belonged together forever.

She climbed on my back with her hands clasped around my neck. We made all sorts of *woo-woo* noises. We laughed like crazy monkeys.

Then my hands slipped on a vine. We fell. I went crashing to the ground. My leg hurt so badly that I could hardly stand on it. Mu-Mu fell on top of my back, so she wasn't hurt.

A villager not far away heard my scream. When he saw me limping and crying, he ran to get my mother. Soon she found Mu-Mu, the frightened little gibbon, and Mubu, the irresponsible big sister, who was in tears. I had broken all my grandfather's rules and almost broken my leg, too.

When my grandfather arrived at the scene he sternly said, "it's time to take the gibbon back to its home."

I screamed my head off.

My grandfather ignored my performance. "Her mother is waiting for her," he said.

"*I'm* her mother!" I cried.

"You don't have the same hair and the same language," he answered calmly.

"Mu-Mu and I *can* talk!" I insisted.

"Oh, so now she has a name?" Grandfather said with a grim look. "Someday, Mubu, you'll see her true home."

Mu-Mu looked worried and also curious as my grandfather carried her away into the forest. Her hand was healed. She didn't need her little doctor anymore. As they disappeared in the trees, I didn't behave very well. I cried very noisily. I could hear my baby hooting for me in the distance.

A couple of months later, Grandfather took me to the forest to see my friend again with her family.

Quietly, hidden in the leaves, we watched them. Mu-Mu had grown larger, but I knew her immediately as she played happily with her brothers and sisters in the trees. Her mother sat on a branch, silently watching them.

Suddenly, I cried out, "*Mu-Mu!*" I couldn't help myself.

Right away, Mu-Mu stopped swinging on her vine and stared in my direction. I was afraid she had forgotten all about me. Maybe to her, I was just another human.

But then she cried, "Woo-woo!" and started hurrying down the vine as she looked in my direction. I looked at my grandfather and didn't dare do any woo-woos myself.

Mu-Mu came running to us, but then she saw I was with my grandfather. She slowed up. All the other gibbons in her family were frightened. They scurried to the tops of the trees.

Somehow my beloved Mu-Mu was clever enough to know not to upset my grandfather. She knew he didn't want any hugging.

Mu-Mu slowly came closer. She touched my hand with her finger as she looked into my eyes.

I smiled. I understood her message. I extended my finger. Our two fingers touched each other. Then my gibbon turned and quietly swung back to her family in the trees.

She *had* remembered me. I would never forget Mu-Mu. The two of us would be soul mates forever.

Soul Mates Forever

Stay in the Tops of the Trees

One of the first things Mu-Mu's mother taught her once Grandfather Noom had returned the gibbon to the forest was "Stay in the tops of the trees."

"You'll be safer that way," she explained. Much of the food Mu-Mu needed could be found in the highest branches, so she seldom needed to come down to the ground where various dangers might lurk.

Mu-Mu ate fruit. She particularly enjoyed figs. Like all gibbons, she also ate leaves, flowers and insects.

It is easy and fun for gibbons to travel through the trees. They have extremely long arms and curved fingers, perfect for grabbing branches and swinging.

Mu-Mu belonged to the family of small apes called the **"black-handed** gibbons." Other families of gibbons living in Thailand are the **white-handed** gibbons, the larger **Siamang** gibbons and a family called the **pileated** gibbons.

Most gibbons live up to 30 years of age if they are not killed by hunters or poachers. However, gibbons in Southeast Asia, like Mu-Mu, are endangered animals, even if they avoid hunters and traps. The great forests in which they live, eat and play are being rapidly cut down by people who want to start farms and plantations. Fifty percent of the gibbons' homes in the trees have been destroyed over the past 45 years.

But while trees last, gibbons such as Mu-Mu's family live the daily life they have always known. Each morning they begin by calling and singing loudly to let all their relatives as well as newcomers know where their home is located. "This is us," their voices say. "This is where we live. Please do not disturb our peace."

If you want to see Mu-Mu playing with her brothers and sisters, you'll have to tilt your head back and gaze up at the top of the trees.

Mu-Mu was a Black-handed Gibbon, whose species is endangered due to loss of habitat.

The White-handed Gibbon seldom comes to the ground, swinging swiftly through the tops of trees.

The Siamang is twice the size of Thailand's other gibbons, and has a throat pouch that allows it to sing loudly.

The playful Pileated Gibbon also loves to sing to its friends.

Mubu's Playground

When Mubu was a young girl she didn't have a television to watch, computer games to play or a telephone to talk to her friends.

Was Mubu bored? Hardly.

She had the wonders of northern Thailand to explore. She had mountains with mysterious caves and glistening waterfalls to discover. Valleys shrouded by mist and fog stirred her imagination. She fished in beautiful rivers with her Grandfather Noom.

She climbed trees to pick fruit and talk to monkeys.

When villagers in northern Thailand had boat races on the rivers, she went with her family to cheer.

Mubu and her funny dog, Fatso, went exploring in the forest. One day she actually met a huge, fierce-looking tiger, but that is a story for another book.

She made friends with the pigs, cows and chickens in her village. She gave them names like Saba, Santi and Chaba. You can read all about them in a future Mubu book. It was very funny the day the baby chicks were born in her bed!

Mubu and her grandfather climbed the tallest mountain in Thailand named Doi Chiang Dao, which gave the girl incredible views of the green world below them.

She and her friends even found dinosaur bones in a cave!

In the spring, the most beautiful orchids bloom in northern Thailand. Their perfume fills the surroundings. That was the kind of air Mubu breathed when she was a girl.

Was Mubu a bored child in northern Thailand?

Never.

Photo credit: Khamu girl • **Gabriela Eddolls**

When Mubu grew up, she became a strong and determined woman who loves animals and has become famous for saving all sorts of Nature's wonders, especially elephants.

Her grown-up name is Sangduen "Lek" Chailert and most days you can find her at Elephant Nature Park, a sanctuary she created in the 1990s. There she has many dogs and cats, water buffalo, cows, a black pony, and more than thirty wonderful elephants.

Lek and her friends have saved most of these friendly animals from lives of loneliness and cruelty. Her park is a haven where the elephants and other animals are free to make friends, choose a family, form small groups, and roam and play throughout the park, living among people who love and respect them.

When Lek was only five years old, Grandfather Noom helped heal a man, saving his life. That grateful man paid Grandfather Noom by giving him an elephant named Tong Kham, which means "Golden One."

Lek grew up with Tong Kham. The girl and the beautiful elephant spent many hours together. Lek's friendship with Tong Kham turned into a lifelong passion. Now people from all over the world come to her park to make friends with elephants.

Maybe someday you can come to Elephant Nature Park, too, and live with the elephants for a few days.

Lek's Personal Message to Young Readers

When I was a very young child living in the mountains of northern Thailand with my family, I spent many happy hours playing outside our little bamboo house watching Nature.

There were no televisions or telephones where I lived in those days, but I was so happy watching all the animals and birds that visited me. There were dogs and cats and pigs and chickens that lived with us in our village. Many colorful birds sang lovely songs in the trees. Sometimes monkeys swung by in the trees around me.

The dogs spoke a different language from the cats, and chickens and pigs stayed among their own families. I was fascinated by the way they acted and the talk they made together. The village animals seemed to understand that the baby girl sitting under the taxi tree was interested in them.

They came to study me. The cat sat and watched me play. The dog came to give me a sniff. The chickens found food in my vicinity. Then they stayed to look. The pigs played nearby, making me laugh. I talked to the animals and they began to understand that I loved them so much. I think they grew fond of the tiny human who had joined their world.

This was just the very beginning of my lifetime with animals. My newest friends also became the snowy owl, the gibbon, a bear, eventually the wonderful elephants, and many others. We loved each other, and from that love came trust and loyalty.

Many of you have enjoyed your own pets, a cat or a dog, a bird, a horse, or another animal. You probably know how much they love and trust you. Some pets have even saved the lives of their owners in the case of fires or other dangers. Many pet owners have risked their own lives to save a pet from disaster.

Pets are not the only animals that deserve your kindness and protection. Animals that live in the shrinking wilderness of our planet now need help more than ever. That is why I spend my life trying to protect elephants, one of the most intelligent and noble animals on Earth.

I would love to hear your stories about animals. About your pets or the animals you have met in the forest. If you have a picture of yourself with your favorite animal, I would love to see it.

Perhaps, if you send me your animal story and picture, Peter will write another book, this time about *your* adventures with animals.

Love,

Lek (Mubu)

Please send your animal stories and pictures

to:

Lek @ Kennebec Entertainment
P.O. Box 7
Trang, 92000, THAILAND

ABOUT THE AUTHOR

Peter Alexander is the author of children's books and a documentary filmmaker with a lifelong interest in the welfare of animals. His film, *The Animals Are Crying*, won many awards and helped schoolchildren learn more about cats and dogs. He has written a new movie screenplay, *The Earth Trembled*, about the plight of a baby Asian elephant and its mother.

Peter lives in Thailand and the United States and counts as among his best friends seven street dogs, numerous cats, two parrots, and the many elephants he has met at Lek Chailert's Elephant Nature Park in northern Thailand.

ABOUT THE ARTIST:

As father of two teenage daughters, illustrator-cartoonist Paulo Sergio of Joinville, Brazil, jumped at the chance to become the artist for Mubu & Mu-Mu: the little animal doctor. "Children need heroes and heroines," Paulo says, "and they don't have to all be adults. Mubu is a super-heroine; she loves animals and will do anything for them. That's the spirit I tried to capture in my illustrations."

In his work for books, comic books, business publications and advertisers during the past 25 years, Paulo has employed a variety of artistic techniques, including watercolor, pastel and acrylics, all within his fully computerized Brazilian art studio